And Then it Rained on Malcolm

Sky Pony Press books may be purchased in bulk at special discounts for sales promotion, corporate gifts, fund-raising, or educational purposes. Special editions can also be created to specifications. For details, contact the Special Sales Department, Sky Pony Press, 307 West 36th Street, 11th Floor, New York, NY 10018 or info@skyhorsepublishing.com.

Sky Pony® is a registered trademark of Skyhorse Publishing, Inc.®, a Delaware corporation.

Visit our website at www.skyponypress.com.

10 9 8 7 6 5 4 3 2 1

Manufactured in China, May 2015
This product conforms to CPSIA 2008

Library of Congress Cataloging-in-Publication Data is available on file.

Cover design by Gretchen Schuler
Cover illustration credit Rich Farr

Print ISBN: 978-1-63450-150-7
Ebook ISBN: 978-1-63450-911-4

And Then it Rained on Malcolm

Written by Paige Feurer
Illustrated by Rich Farr

Sky Pony Press
New York

It rained on Malcolm's
town.

It rained on Malcolm's
street.

It rained on
Malcolm's house.

And then it rained on Malcolm.

At first, young Malcolm sulked.

At first, young
Malcolm yelled.

At first, young
Malcolm scowled.

And then came his idea.

He put on his red boots.

He put on his red coat.

He put on his red hat.

And then put on his goggles.

He splashed around
the steps.

He splashed around
the yard.

He splashed around
the dog.

And then he jumped in puddles.

The worms got in
his boots.

The worms got in
his coat.

The worms got in
his hair.

And then they started tickling.

He ran right through
the mud.

He ran right through
the sand.

He ran right through
the house.

And then he got in trouble.

He looked at all
the muck.

He looked at all
the filth.

He looked at all
the mess.

And then knew how to fix it.

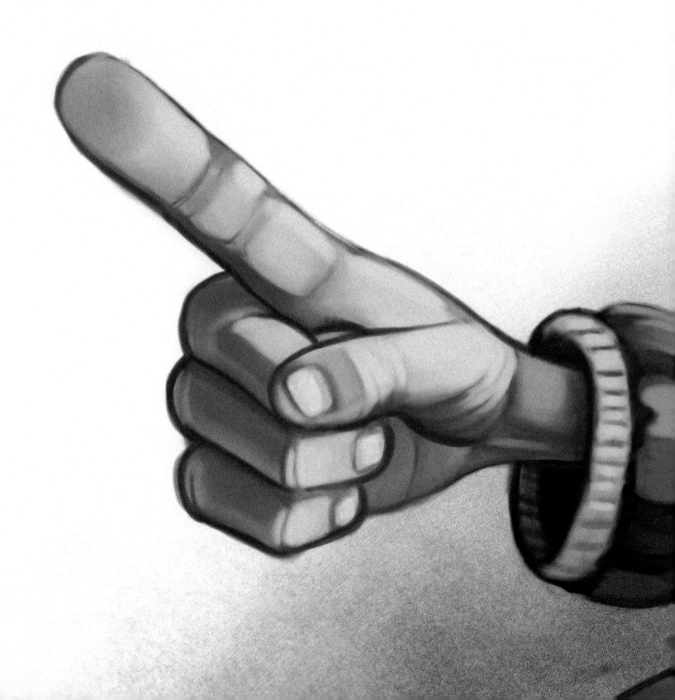

He gathered up
his clothes.

He gathered up
his dog.

He gathered up his worms.

And then he found
a rainstorm.

For Avery and Quinn. Love you, love you, love you.
Always, always will. Rain or shine.
- P. F.

For Connor and Ethan, who inspire me
to splash in puddles whenever possible.
- R. F.